Hotwife Fantasy Comes True - A Steamy Romance Hot Wife Novel

Karly Violet

Published by Karly Violet, 2021.

This is a work of fiction. Similarities to real people, places, or events are entirely coincidental.

HOTWIFE FANTASY COMES TRUE - A STEAMY ROMANCE HOT WIFE NOVEL

First edition. March 22, 2021.

Copyright © 2021 Karly Violet.

ISBN: 979-8201045647

Written by Karly Violet.

Hotwife Fantasy Comes True
A Steamy Romance Hot Wife Novel

Sign up to my Patreon account and receive exclusive Hotwife stories every month and sexy scenes every week!

https://www.patreon.com/karlyviolet

Chapter One: Dipping the Cock

Sophie always resists a little when I do something this crazy with her, but I have learned how to be gentle while convincing her that something is a good idea. Still, she seems a little worried that someone might see what we are doing as I slide my cock past her lime green bikini bottom and into her soft, wet pussy.

"Dammit, Ollie," she worries while looking around the beach. "There are dozens of people all around us. Someone will see what you are doing if you're not careful."

I relax behind her on the blanket underneath the large umbrella as I slowly thrust in and out of her soft snatch. "Relax, baby," I tell her as I enjoy the tightness of her vagina. "You know we can do this without anyone knowing. We've done it before, right?" I grip her hips tightly as I move a little quicker in and out of her muff. Though she continues to worry, I know that the likelihood that we will be found out by someone on the beach is nearly zero. Whenever I buy new swim trunks, I make certain that they have a velcro fly in the front for easy access to my cock. This feature makes it easy to screw my beautiful Sophie on the beach even though there are other people around.

"Someone will see," she laments again as she tries to steady her body. My balls ache as I feel myself getting closer to losing my wad inside Sophie. "I can't believe you sometimes, Oliver Cooke." My wife adjusts her sunglasses and tries to pretend to be looking at her cell phone as I move a little faster. I am close right now and about to pop inside her warm snapper. The thought that there are other beachgoers around makes the experience that much more exciting as I grip her hips tightly.

"Fuck, honey. *Uhhhh...*"

"*Shhhh!*" Sophie turns to give me a stern look as I begin to come inside her. I want to yell out as I orgasm, but I also realize all too well that doing so would probably cause the other people on the beach to walk up and see what we are up to. The county sheriff's department patrols the beach and there is a zero tolerance rule concerning nudity or sexual activity in public. If we were to be caught, it would certainly mean a stiff fine and possibly a little jail time for the both of us.

"Ohhh..." I press my face into my wife's back as I finish off inside her. It is not much longer before I pull out of her and she reaches down to adjust her bikini bottoms.

"That's disgusting, Ollie," she tells me as she wipes her hand on a towel nearby. "I'm dripping with it and someone will probably see. You shouldn't have done this to me on the beach again."

"Didn't you like it?" I ask with a chuckle as I adjust myself inside my trunks before closing up the fly.

Sophie turns to face me on the blanket. "No, I didn't come, did I? How could I enjoy having sex in public in front of people? You have made a mess all over me down there and it's leaking out of me. Someone will probably notice the mess soon." She turns and looks at a small group of young men nearby who have been looking our way. They are obviously attracted to my beautiful, petite wife of only thirty-two years old. Sophie's dark brown hair accentuates her blue eyes and warm, dark red lips as she turns back to face me. I get a slight woody as I see the look on her face.

"You know that they know, right?"

"Shit, I hope not," she replies as her face turns a little red. "You shouldn't do that to me on the beach, Ollie. It's disgusting and a little dirty. The sand is all around and it would be irritating if it gets inside there."

"The sand?" I laugh. "That's why we have a blanket. Besides, you are just worried that they might know what I just did with you. It turns me on a little, to be honest."

Sophie frowns. "Yeah, well, it shouldn't," she chastises me. "Most husbands wouldn't like other men looking at their wives, Ollie. What if one of them were to come over here and make some kind of off-color comment to me about my body? Would you still find it a turn on then?" She focuses her blue eyes on me and I think back to when I met her just ten years ago. We had both just finished our stint at the same university without having met each other while there. Though it seemed at first that my future wife was not interested in me when we met, she soon became a fiery sexual animal with me in bed to the point that I thought I was dreaming. Thankfully, I was not, and we got married about a year later. I have not regretted one moment of my marriage to Sophie, though I cannot be certain that she could say the same.

"Those guys are just horny college dudes," I reply. "They're pretty harmless for the most part. As a matter of fact, I was a lot like them back in the day."

"Back in the day," Sophie laughs while raising an eyebrow. "You've only been out for a decade, Oliver. It's not as if you are an old man and over the hill, you know."

"No, I've still got it," I chuckle. "Maybe that's why I like to give you a little something once in a while when we come out here." Patting her hip, I smile wickedly at my wife. "You've still got it too, my love. That's why I like doing this sort of thing so much with you."

Her face blushes a little as she smiles. "If we ever get caught, I'm going to plead insanity. I don't want to go to jail for beach sex, sweetheart. You shouldn't want to either."

I shrug my shoulders. "It's fun, though. I know you didn't get off, but you were excited about it too, weren't you? Your eyes betrayed the way you were feeling about it while I fucked you, baby." I lean forward and kiss her hard before she pushes me away, giggling.

"You are a nasty man," Sophie tells me with a grin. "But I suppose you are just a little right. I do like the way you enjoy me whenever you want to. I just wish you would find a safer way to do it instead of in front of other people. It makes me really nervous to be in front of people while doing that."

"A safer way? Do you mean like the way a lot of old people have sex? Go to the bedroom, lock the door, and hope that no one knows that you actually have sex sometimes? Is that the *safe* way you want?" I reach forward and run a finger over the outline of my wife's nipple through the soft material of her bikini top. Her body reacts a little before she pushes my hand away with hers.

"Don't," Sophie says quietly. "Someone will see you. The beach is starting to get crowded now." She looks over my shoulder and nods her head. I turn to see a young family setting up just a few feet away.

"Shit," I laugh quietly as I look back at her. "I'm glad they didn't walk up while we were having sex just a few minutes ago."

"Yeah, that would have been really bad. You would have scarred those young children for life." We both laugh quietly before leaning in and kissing each other for a moment. I love Sophie so much that I cannot help but enjoy her company anywhere we go. However, I also lust for my wife to the point that sometimes I make unwise decisions about how I will behave around her. Pulling her bottoms to the side and having sex with her on the beach near strangers is something that I probably should avoid doing again in the near future. Sometimes I feel as if I simply cannot help myself, though. I just want her.

"How is work at the shop?" I ask Sophie as I lean on my elbow.

She nods her head and smiles. "Things are fine, I suppose. You know how hard it can be to get businesses to buy printed materials nowadays, though. Even convincing some of them to buy business cards has become really hard." My wife inherited a print shop from her parents when they decided to retire early to enjoy their vacation home in Washington state. Reggie and Caroline are great in-laws and love being around us when they are back here in Florida, but they love the mountains of the northwest even more. Sophie and I figure they will soon sell their home here and make the move more permanent.

"Just don't give up," I tell her. "You know I'll help in any way that I can, right? You and I are partners in crime, after all."

Sophie smirks. "Yeah, especially a few minutes ago. Let's see, there is public indecency, public sex acts, lewd offense to minors..."

"What the hell?" I interrupt as I laugh. "Did you look that all up, my love?"

"Maybe." My wife raises an eyebrow and smiles. "I should probably just sell off the business and design websites or something like that. My degree in graphic design is just not cutting it with the print shop. I had hoped there would have been more companies willing to hire me for sign design and corporate logos. Apparently there are much cheaper options overseas."

"And those options suck balls," I reply. "You know you're better than that cheap shit some of those places are putting out. Some of the local companies have discovered that already and started to buy more from you, right?"

She nods her head. "Well, sure, some of them, but it's still pretty tight, Ollie. Each month is a squeaker when I balance the books and sometimes I wonder if we might have to actually pay in to keep things even."

"Did you pay yourself this month?" I ask.

Sophie shakes her head. "We cleared just over three thousand dollars, so I didn't think that it would be a good idea to do so. I've been putting the extra money back in the bank just in case we need it to cover expenses or to pay the staff." My wife has three people who work for her at the shop, and all of them were hired by her parents. Though at one time the shop turned a very nice profit and enriched her family to some degree, the last five years have sapped a lot of the business. Online graphics needs have taken over a lot of the market due to the cheaper nature of the work. Of course, if someone is paying people in the Philippines just a dollar per hour to do the same work to design and then print the products, it becomes hard to compete on an honest level here at home.

"You know that I can carry us indefinitely on my income," I remind her. "You can just take your time with the business and when things get better they get better. That's all there is to it."

My wife smiles and kisses me once more before replying, "I knew there was a reason I married a pervert like you."

I shake my head as I laugh. "Well, this beach pervert loves you very much and will do anything to help you get things off the ground with the shop, Sophie. I hope you know that."

"I do." We kiss again and this time we lie down side by side on the blanket together. As we hold hands, we go to sleep in the shade of the large umbrella on the Florida coast. I love Sophie so much and I want to do whatever I can to help her fulfill her dreams. She has done so much for me, after all, including allowing me to have sex with her in public. A woman like that deserves whatever she desires in life.

Chapter Two: A Sexy Wife

My job as a sales account manager for a major retailer has allowed me to become fairly successful as I have stoked what appears to be a good working relationship with the executives upstairs. It has also been nice to work in an office next door to an old college chum, Todd Dunigan. He is the human resources manager and was the one who tipped me off to the spot in management at the corporate office three years ago. Since moving in, we have both shared practically everything about our private lives with each other, which is odd when considering that we rarely see each other outside work.

"How's the old ball and chain?" he asks with a chuckle as he sits down in the chair in front of my desk.

Shaking my head, I reply, "Sophie is great. How has your love life been lately?"

"Ow, a *zinger!*" Todd laughs while shaking his head. "You do realize that you are married to the future Mrs. Todd Dunigan, right? Surely you can't imagine that I would let you keep her forever. You're just keeping her warm for me until I'm ready to settle down and have kids." There is a strange guffaw that always drops from my old friend's mouth anytime he talks about my wife this way. Though it might cause most men to become very uncomfortable with the topic of conversation, it bothers me very little. I know Todd and the way he likes to joke around with me and my marriage to Sophie. He means no harm by it and never crosses the line with me when he talks about her this way. However, I am not certain that he knows where the line actually is.

"You know, you should try to get out more, man. There are a lot of young women in the world who would be willing to spend some time with the great Todd Dunigan."

He shakes his head while looking at me. "Hook me up with Sophie's sister, Ollie. You know I would love to go on a date with her, right?"

"You know that Sophie doesn't have a sister, Todd. It's just the one brother."

"Really? I thought she had an identical twin sister?" He looks at me for a moment before adding, "Damn, buddy, that boner I keep getting for the woman who looks like her must be...for *her*." He laughs hard as I shake my head once again. Smiling, I begin to laugh with Todd as I think about his perverted mind. We spent a lot of time at keg parties in college together and he was exactly the same back then. His jokes are irreverent and borderline personally intrusive. His humor is tasteless and very sharp at times, causing some of his own friends to cringe when they hear some of the foul commentary that comes from his mouth. Even so, Todd is a very likable guy. He is the sort of friend that will come to your aid no matter what is going on and back you up no matter how wrong you might be. This man is the man you want in the foxhole with you, if you end up in one. A good friend, I enjoy being around Todd, even if he makes sexual comments about my wife every single day.

"Sophie hates you, Todd. You do know that, right?" I raise an eyebrow while sitting back in my chair. "She absolutely hates you."

My old friend nods his head. "I figured that she might. That's why you need to smooth things over with her for me. Don't leave me hanging with her, Ollie."

"You can't keep your mouth shut," I remind him. "The times that you have been around her you have said some things that you should have just been kept between us."

"Well, maybe you shouldn't have told me about that time you walked in on her mother in the shower naked." Todd laughs as he sits back in his chair. "I think she was more pissed at you than at me."

I sigh as I smile. "I told you about that in confidence. You know that you can't just go to a guy's wife and tell her that her husband got a good look at her mother in the nude, Todd. That's pretty common sense stuff." We both laugh, though I feel a little uneasy now to confide in my college chum as much as I once did. It is true that I saw Caroline, Sophie's fifty-year-old mother, standing in our shower last year. My wife had failed to mention to me before I got home that Caroline would be staying with us for a couple of weeks and that she would be without a car. I assumed at the time that Sophie had gotten home early and wanted a shower. I also assumed that my friskiness would be met with a warm greeting and maybe some oral love when I walked into the bathroom with nothing on, along with a massive hardon, before pulling the curtain back to find my mother-in-law standing there in the nude. She froze. She fucking froze. While looking down at my cock, Caroline simply stood there in our shower, the water slowly running down her perky breasts as she took in the sight of my manhood. Of course, I froze as well as I let her look me over. It took several moments for me to slowly back away and leave the bathroom behind as the image of her freshly shaved snapper kept scrolling through my mind. I had seen my wife's mother naked, and I liked it a bit too much.

"Look, I've got your back if you ever need a place to stay, man. Just let me know when the time comes."

"Yeah, I'll do that." I raise an eyebrow as I smile wryly at Todd. "So, how are things in the personnel office?"

"Good, I guess," he replies. "I had to fire a lady just a couple of days ago. She was stealing company stuff."

"Like what?"

"The usual," he answers. "She found out that it wasn't all that difficult to get into the storeroom downstairs and so she started carrying out some things that didn't belong to her. The sad thing is, I fired her for taking a few manila envelopes and an electric pencil sharpener. We don't even use that shit around here much anymore."

I nod my head. "You couldn't have given her a warning instead of tossing her out?"

"Nah. The bosses upstairs caught her on video. Had I been the one who had caught her, it might have turned out differently. Unfortunately for her, they aren't all that forgiving in the executive offices if you take from the company. She was a goner before she even knew it." Todd looks out the window nearby. "Now, had she been more attractive..."

"Oh, geesh, man," I say with a chuckle as I shake my head. "You seriously don't do shit like that, right? If you do, one of these days someone will take you to court over it."

"I cannot confirm nor deny the existence of any cell phone video recordings of women trying to save their jobs," he tells me with a grin on his face.

"You are out of your mind, Todd."

"Yes, but I get laid a lot more than you do, bro."

"Seriously? We're back to my wife again?"

"Look, man, she's hot. Everyone here knows how hot Sophie is. Hell, I would bet that there is an exec or two upstairs beating off to security footage of her coming in and out of this building. When you are married to someone like that, you have to know that there will be other men ogling her, Ollie." Todd moves around in his seat a little and I realize that he is trying to adjust a hardon in his pants. Though it makes me a little horny to think about other men wanting to fuck my wife, it sometimes gets tiring. He is absolutely right, though. The other men in our building have noticed Sophie the few times that she has come by to pick me up for lunch or to drop something off for me. They talk about the women who come here, and even some of the women here talk. It is something that I have come to understand that I cannot control. And I am fine with that. For the most part.

"You need to get off my wife," I tell him.

Todd's face turns red as he explodes into laughter. "Not until I'm *finished*." He laughs even harder as he leans back in his seat. I realized as soon as the request had left my lips that I had made a *faux pas* of the sexual variety. As quick-witted as my old friend happens to be, he never allows such things to get past him.

"Alright, alright. Seriously, man." I give him a stern look as I sit forward in my chair. Todd understands that even I have my limits when it comes to joking around about Sophie. So, he nods his head and tries to contain his laughter.

"Sorry, man," he says after a moment of calm. "You know how I can be, and after having three cups of coffee this morning I'm in rare form."

"I'll say," I reply. "Anyway, we have that meeting with the upstairs people later this afternoon. I'm guessing that the personnel office has to attend as well?"

Todd rolls his eyes. "Yeah, I got the memo too. I wish they would stop calling us in like this. So the company's going to hell in a handbasket? We can't do anything about it down here."

"It's not that bad," I tell my old friend. "I'm still buying inventory like it's Christmas and we are selling things in high volume in our stores. I think we'll be alright in the near future."

"Until the company is bought out and we end up without jobs. There are three major chains gunning for us, Ollie. Even that big blue box store wants our asses."

I smile. "You need to stop with the conspiracy theories, dude. It's getting old as hell. We're good. Management just wants us to keep the belts tightened so that things remain good." Everything Todd worries about has some basis in reality. The third quarter of last year saw a sudden decline in sales that temporarily put our company in the red for the first time in its half-century history. That spooked some of our investors, who then began to sell off their stock in earnest. As stock prices dropped, there was commentary on several major network television news programs that we were going under. We were all worried, but the executives of the company took a heavy hand in making sure that we were fiscally secure. Things are better, but for many who work here there is still the threat of suddenly losing a job.

"Hey, things will go downhill eventually," Todd replies. "Just like people, companies eventually die. This one is no exception."

"Well, not today." I take a breath before asking, "Are we still on for Saturday?"

"The golf thing?" Todd nods his head. "Sure. I'll be there by eight."

"Fuck, man," I chuckle. "Eight in the *morning?* Why not eleven like last time?"

"It's too damn hot," my friend complains. "If we go out at eight we will be finished before eleven and then we can then go get something to eat and drink. I think I want a tall beer at that one place near the golf course."

"The German place?" I nod my head. "Yeah, that does sound good. I guess I can do eight, but my swing will suck the first half-hour or so."

"I'm counting on it," Todd says with a smile as he gets up from the chair where he has been sitting. "I'll see you later, Ollie. Have a good one."

"You too." I stand to my feet as well and watch as he leaves my office to go back to his own office. I am amazed at the friendship that we have and the things that we talk about whenever we get together. Todd Dunigan is a good friend and I enjoy his company, but I will never again be able to invite him to my house for dinner or a party. Not after he told Sophie that I told him about seeing Caroline naked in the shower. No, it will be a cold day in Palm Springs when that happens again, all thanks to Todd's big mouth.

Chapter Three: Hardly a Novel

The stories often get me pretty hard whenever I write them, though this post is especially naughty in nature. "My wife is the kind of slut who can run her velvet hand over the stiff cock of any gentleman three times and cause him to come like a genie popping out of a magical lamp," I say quietly to myself as I read the short story to myself. Chuckling, I lean back in my chair and add, "I'm no Lewis Carroll or Ray Bradbury, but I can whip out a naughty tale quickly and efficiently." I have been writing on an adult message board about my own fantasies involving my wife for the last few months. It is something that I do to help curb some of the intense sexual desires I feel toward Sophie and the desire that I have to see her in bed with another man. Sexy and very alluring, my wife has one characteristic that seems to challenge anyone's first impressions of her; she's very prudish in many respects of the word.

"She's not a sexual deviant by anyone's standards," I laugh to myself as I think about her. I love my wife with all my heart, but just once I wish she would actually entertain the idea of fucking some other man while I watch. We have a good sex life, but I want a *great* one, and unfortunately Sophie just is not as interested as I am in being sexually active with another man. She is shy and somewhat of an introvert sometimes, and that just does not help my case when I make such dirty little suggestions in bed with her.

My desk telephone rings and I pick it up. "Still here?" Todd says with a chuckle on the other end of the line.

"Yeah, I'm just finishing up some things," I reply. "There's some work that still needs to be wrapped up before I leave."

"Damn, you are a busy man." My friend laughs on the other end before adding, "I'm heading out now. I was just checking to see if you want to hit the bar with me for a while and tie one on."

"No, I'm good," I reply. "We can enjoy a few beers together when we go golfing over the weekend."

"You're buying."

"Me? It's your turn, buddy."

Todd sighs. "Dammit, dude, have you already forgotten? I beat you on the last hole when we played golf last month. The deal was that you would buy drinks the next time."

"Ah, shit," I say with a laugh as I recall my poor performance on the last golf hole when we last went to the golf course. "Yeah, okay. I'll cover drinks."

"You should cover lunch too, bro." I get the feeling Todd is smiling on the other end of the line.

"Nah, you can buy your own damned hamburger." We both laugh before I continue, "Hey, let me go, okay? I need to wrap this up and get out of here. I promised to take Sophie to dinner tonight and I don't want to be late getting home."

"Ah, the seductive Sophie," Todd sighs. "Give her a kiss and a poke for me, pal."

"Shit, man." We laugh again as my friend and coworker hangs up the phone. I put my desk phone receiver back into its cradle and sit back in my desk as I look up at the computer screen. "Just a few more lines." Leaning forward, I continue typing on the short story that I will post in the adult forum online. Since becoming a member on this site, I have read dozens of stories and posted many of my own, developing a following of nearly a hundred readers. There is no money to be gained by posting here, but there is certainly something to be said for having strangers read about your deepest fantasies concerning your wife.

Moving my computer mouse, I place the finished story into an email folder and save it for distribution to my list of subscribers later. There are still a few corrections I hope to make before I send it off for other men to enjoy, along with a link to where it will post online. Then, standing up from my chair behind my desk, I reach for my jacket and make my way toward the office door.

"I'll see you tomorrow, Rachel," I say to the young woman in the main lobby moments later.

She looks up at me, her dark brown eyes lighting up as she smiles at me. "Have a good evening, Oliver. I'll see you bright and early in the morning." Rachel nods at me and turns back to her work as I walk out of the building's main doors.

"Fucking nice," I say to myself with a smile. Rachel is in her early twenties and quite possibly one of the most attractive women I have ever known besides my wife. Sure, I would love to bang her, but the fact of the matter is we are both married. Fucking each other would likely lead to something dire in our marital relationships. Besides, Todd has told me on more than one occasion that I have exactly zero chance with the young receptionist. I beg to differ, but still, I do not want to attempt to make a move on her.

My cell phone rings as I make my way to my car. "Hey, baby," I say to my wife.

"Hey, Ollie," she replies cheerfully. "Don't forget our little dinner date tonight, alright? I've been looking forward to it all day."

I smile. "Me too. As a matter of fact, I can't wait to serve you dessert afterward."

"Oh, sweetheart," she moans with a giggle. "As long as that dessert doesn't require me to be on the beach in front of other people eating it."

Laughing, I reply, "You're still simmering over that?"

"I'm not simmering," she replies a little defensively. "Just don't ask me to do that sort of thing in public again. I still think there were people watching us."

"And so what if they were?"

"So what? Ollie, that was not something that I enjoy doing."

"I know, you didn't come. I need to do something about that tonight, don't I?" I feel my cock becoming hard as I pull my car keys from my pocket and press the button to unlock my car.

"Not in public." My wife's tone is very flat and decisive as she says this to me.

"You know that I won't do anything stupid at the restaurant, honey," I reply. "I promise."

"Good, because I'm not giving you oral there or anywhere else in public. However, if you want something like that, I can probably arrange for it at home as long as you are a good boy while we are eating out."

My dirty mind takes the last two words of her statement and turns them into a fantasy of their own as I think about Sophie on a restaurant table with her legs spread open for another man to eat her out. I can never help myself when I begin to think about such things.

"I'll be good," I promise. "Cross my heart."

"Good." I can tell that this has put a smile on my sexy wife's face. "Then I'll see you at home soon? You'll need to change before we leave, after all. We're going to get barbecue."

"Barbecue?" I scrunch my nose as I think about Sophie's choice of restaurant. I had hoped for Thai or even Chinese food tonight.

"Just tonight. Wear a button up shirt and a pair of jeans. We don't want to show up in our work outfits."

"Okay." I pout slightly before asking, "Is there anything I need to pick up along the way? I'll probably be passing the grocery store."

"Sure, maybe get us a little wine for after we get home? That would be nice, wouldn't it? To enjoy a little chilled wine in our living room?" Sophie giggles a little on the other end of the line.

"Yeah, that would be very nice," I concur as I start my car and begin to pull out into the street. "I'll see you in about a half-hour, baby."

"I'll see you then, sexy man." Sophie hangs up and I drop my cell phone into the cup holder beside me. She sometimes calls me her sexy man whenever she is a little horny. Maybe there will be a little action tonight between the two of us after dinner. Maybe I will even be able to get her to put on the sexy little outfit that I got her last Christmas. My wife has yet to wear it, feeling that the French maid look is too overused sexually. Though I tend to agree somewhat, I think it would look fantastic on her.

"You're getting some tonight," I say to myself with a laugh as I sit back in my car seat and just drive. "Sophie is going to be all over you, Ollie. You had better be ready." With a smile on my face, I drive all the way back home. It is sometimes funny how a person can think that they are about to have one hell of a night with their wife when in fact that is not to be the case at all.

Chapter Four: A Huge Mistake

I walk into our house and immediately see Sophie sitting on the sofa in the living room. "Hey," I say as I smile at her. The smile is not quickly returned as I stand just inside the doorway of our home.

My wife sighs and frowns a little. "Ollie, you know that I have put up with a lot of things in our marriage that are a little over the top sometimes, right?"

Shaking my head, I take a seat beside her and ask, "What do you mean?"

Sophie sighs for a second time. "I mean exactly what I just said. There have been some things that I have had to overlook with our marriage just to get things to work the way they should. I thought you had more respect for me than this."

I chuckle nervously. What is she talking about? Did I say something on the phone earlier when we spoke that upset her? Was there some *faux pas* that passed my lips and shouldn't have? Occasionally, my wife will attempt to test my attitude about something we have been talking about. These tests are a way for her to get a sense of my thinking on some topic that she finds important. Though I often play along without any problems, this line of questioning seems a bit sharper than normal.

"Alright," I say as I lean back in my seat. "What did I do this time, my love?"

Crossing her arms, Sophie stares hard at me. I feel a cold chill run down my neck and back as she replies, "You sent it to everyone on your damned email list, Ollie. How the hell could you be so fucking careless...or *rude?*" A few tears fill her eyes as she shakes her head slowly.

"Honey, I don't know what you are..."

"*This.*" She hands me her cell phone. On the screen is her email account and an apparent email sent from me a little earlier. "Go on. Click the link." I do and suddenly I find myself on the same adult forum where I have written several stories about Sophie. My heart suddenly skips several beats as I try to think of what to say to my wife next.

"I'm *Sophia,* right? Isn't that me?"

"Sophie, I..."

"Don't you even try to explain this shit away," she fires at me with a sharp tongue. "You know what you've done, Oliver. You know very well what you have done." She shakes her head and takes a quick breath before continuing, "Do you really write about me and what you want me to do with other men? That's fucking embarrassing."

My mind scurries to come up with something to counter her with, but I have nothing. The fact of the matter is, I have spent the last several months writing dirty little stories about what I would like to see done with and to my beautiful young wife. Though we have talked about our fantasies at length, Sophie has often blunted whatever I have said by calling my thoughts "disgusting" or "weird." There are lots of men who fantasize about their wives and girlfriends having sex with other men, and oftentimes those women are glad to at least play along during sex with them. Not my chosen mate. No, she refuses to even pretend about such things in the privacy of our own home. It is the very reason that I have found myself writing on the forums. The thought of other men reading and getting off to my fantasies has in turn given me some sexual relief. Of course, this is often at my own hands in the bathroom very late at night.

"How did you get that?" I query as I begin to temper my response.

Sophie wipes an eye with her hand before replying, "You sent it to me this afternoon about the time we spoke on the phone. Why would you send that to me?" Again, a chill runs along my spine. I had intended to save the work in my email to post tomorrow, but apparently something went wrong and everything posted immediately. Damn my inability to focus at the end of a long work day!

"Baby, I didn't mean to send that to you. It's just a joke."

"A *joke?!*" Sophie takes her phone from me and opens up the contacts in the email. "Every fucking person in your email contacts list got it, Ollie! What are they thinking now that they know that you write this shit about me? They probably think that I'm a slut. They probably think that I'm some common whore who does your bidding with whatever man you bring over to the house. Fuck, Ollie. *FUCK!*" She recoils from me as I reach out for her. I begin to worry what damage I may have done to our marriage at this point.

"I can't explain my way out of this, honey. I know that. Please just understand that I write these stories as a way to help alleviate some of the pressures of the workday for me. It's nothing against you and honestly I didn't think about the fact that the character's name is so similar to yours."

"Fucking lies," my wife hisses. "Fucking lies with you all the time, Oliver. Why do you lie? Why do you take me for some idiot who will simply believe your lies? You did this to get back at me, didn't you? You wanted to make me pay for the way I have resisted your fantasies."

I shake my head. "Please don't put this off on you, Sophie."

"Oh, I'm not," she retorts. "It's definitely not *my* fault that you have a perverted sense of what love looks like. This is all on you, Oliver Cooke."

"*Perverted* sense of love? Sophie, love and sex can be a very separate thing if you want it to be. You don't have to be in love to have sex with other people."

"*There it is!*" she says while sitting forward on the sofa. "Finally, the truth. This whole thing was about me and what you want me to do but I won't do. You are writing this shit about me behind my back. Now everyone on your email mailing list will see it."

"But, most of them don't even know who you are, honey."

She turns to look at me. "Todd Dunigan is on your email address list, Ollie. He knows me and he already has perverted ideas about me. Remember that party and what he said about my mother?"

"Shit." I suddenly realize that my wife is right. Todd is on my list, as are a lot of other people at the company. "I'll talk to him. He won't say anything, Sophie."

"Say anything?! He's probably at home masturbating to your stories about me right now!" Sophie gets up from the sofa and begins to pace the floor in front of the sofa. My heart races as I think about how bad things appear to be for me. She could leave me. My wife could absolutely pack her bags and leave me tonight. "There's no way to get that email back. All those fucking stories on that website that you wrote are now open to everyone we know."

"Baby..."

"Don't do that!" Sophie stops at the window and looks out at the street outside. The silhouette of her sexy body is outlined by the afternoon light that shines through. My wife is a beautiful woman, one that any man would love to spend time with in the bedroom. Oh, why did I have to write those stories? How did I send the link to everyone in my email address book?

"How can I make this up to you? I don't know what to do, Sophie."

"I don't know what you can do either." She sighs as she continues to look out the window while twirling the pendant around her neck with her fingers. "This is way beyond anything that you have done so far, Ollie. This is going to take some time to figure you." She turns to look at me. "You have really embarrassed me, dammit. What if my parents see that link? What happens then?"

"I don't think I have their email addresses in my system at work."

"You have my *brother's.*" The comment causes us both to sit and just stare at each other for a moment as it sinks in.

"Shit, honey. I'm so sorry. I will contact Brad and let him know this was all a joke or something. He's pretty easy going about things."

"He'll tell Mom," she replies solemnly. "He tells her everything. They will both read that smut you have written about me and then I'll never be able to look anyone in the eyes ever again. Thanksgiving will be a lot different from now on, thanks to you."

I feel a little nauseous as I promise, "I'll go in tonight and clear everything out of the forums. All of the stories will be gone when I'm finished. My account will be deleted as well."

"It should have never existed," Sophie complains softly. "You have really screwed me over this time. Dammit, Ollie. Why do you push those fantasies on me so much? What's wrong with you that you have to constantly be thinking of me with other men? Can't our marriage and sex life be enough for you without bringing other men into it?"

"They're just fantasies," I reply in my defense. "The sort of fantasies that lots of men have about their wives. It's not like I'm a sick predator or something like that. We're married and I sometimes like to think about you with other men."

"But then you write about it for other people to see and read and think about. That's really wrong, Oliver."

I shake my head. "Look, I admit that I royally screwed up by sending out the link to everyone like that, but it's not such a strange thing to fantasize about. You can be just a little prudish when I mention these things during sex, so the stories have become a way for me to get some kind of relief."

Sophie narrows her eyes and points a finger at me. "Don't you dare try to put this off on me, Oliver. Dammit, why are you like this? Why do you always try to flip these things so that I sound like the bad guy? I don't like your fantasies. They're not okay."

"And I haven't asked you to like them. All I have ever asked is for you to play along during sex. You can't even do that with me, honey. I'm your husband and I want to have some fun with you, but I often feel that I can't because you are so stuck up on yourself and whatever image you have of yourself that you have conjured up in your mind. Fuck, honey, I feel like I'm suffocating in our sex life." The words should have never passed my lips, but here they are, hanging in the air between us as once again our argument begins to heat up.

"You're a fucking asshole," Sophie barks at me. "You don't care about me and my feelings. All you want is to make *him* happy." She points at my pants where my pecker is put away. "It's all about whether you get off."

"I haven't seen you complain whenever he helps *you* get off," I say in reference to my own cock. "Seriously, Sophie, you are being a little too uptight about this whole thing. When we get back from dinner I will delete everything on the account. Most of the people who got the email probably haven't seen it yet anyway. I'll tell them all that a virus was in my system and it sent out the link without my permission. You'll be completely exonerated as the prim and perfect little wife you try to make yourself out to be." I can feel myself seethe a little as I shake my head and get up from where I am sitting. If our marriage is going to go down in flames over this, I might as well pour plenty of gasoline onto it.

"We're not going out to eat," my wife replies flatly. "And we are also not going to sleep together tonight. You can have the sofa." She turns and walks back toward our bedroom. The door slams behind her as I stand and watch in disillusionment.

"Fuck me," I groan as I run my hands over my head. "You're a real idiot, Ollie. A real fucking idiot. All you had to do was make sure to check that the email for tomorrow was set for *tomorrow* and addressed correctly. No one in my normal list should have gotten the email, but I apparently checked the wrong box before closing my email account. It should have gone out tomorrow to a select group of people who subscribe to my forum threads. "Sophie will make you pay for this, man. You are really going to suffer by the time she is finished with you." My wife and I have had arguments before, but none as deep as this one. We have argued over our sex life and she has often told me that I expect more than I should. After all, she's not a whore or a slut, right? It doesn't matter that I am her husband.

"I hope Todd doesn't see it," I say as I pull my cell phone out of my pocket and go to my account on the forums. I begin the process of trying to dismantle the dozen or so stories I have posted there. If everything works out correctly, I will be able to report to Sophie tomorrow that there has been minimal damage done. Keeping this sort of stuff away from my friend at work will likely be the big thing in Sophie's mind. He is, after all, a bit of a horny asshole. I do worry that if he sees it he might say something to my wife at some point in the future. "Maybe not," I reassure myself as I try to remember my password and other credentials to gain access to my account information on the website. "He won't say anything. He's my friend."

Chapter Five: Fallout

"Fucking hell," I complain as I sit at my desk at work. Only just now am I able to delete the last post on my forum account. All night long I tried to remember my password so that I could do this at home on my cell phone. Unfortunately, I only used my work computer to write the stories, where the browser there saved my login information. It wasn't until eight this morning that I could get into the building to make my way to the computer to expunge the world wide web of the stories I have written about Sophie's alter-ego, Sophia.

"Knock knock," Todd says as he opens the door to my office and sticks his head inside. "I've come to say hello this morning." I wave him inside and he walks up to my desk to have a seat directly across from me. "How are things today, my friend?"

I shrug my shoulders as I think about the earnest effort I have been involved in over the last hour. "Things could be better, but I'm making it. How about for you?"

He smiles. "My day has been pretty good. You know, I've been upstairs for the last half-hour talking about hiring and firing. I'm going to have to let Steve Landers in accounting go this afternoon." He leans forward and adds, "Don't tell him, though. It's meant to be a little surprise." My friend allows a wicked smile to spread across his face.

"What happened? More cutbacks?"

"Nah, he just got caught surfing cyberporn last week, that's all. Management has decided they don't want to be tied to that, so they're going to dump the guy at the end of the day."

I swallow hard as I think of my own issues. "After eight years?"

"Ten," Todd corrects me. "Ten years of hard work and dedicated service. He's gone this afternoon." He shakes his head. "I wonder what he was thinking by using his office computer? Surely he knew that we would see that he was viewing porn during his workday."

"Yeah, that's a little careless," I reply.

"He could have avoided it all by just searching for that at home and watching it there, but I hear his wife would have exploded on him.

Just wait until she discovers her husband has lost his job over that sort of thing. *Youch.*" Todd shakes his head and chuckles. "You know, there have been some others who have been really good at keeping the IT department from finding out about their own sexual gratification online. If only Steve would have done it the same way. I wouldn't be letting him go this afternoon if that had been the case."

I feel my heart in my throat as I attempt to understand what my friend is saying. "Just come out with it," I finally tell him as he continues to stare at me.

"Is it true?" Todd asks. "Has Sophie been doing the things you wrote about in those stories in that forum?"

"*Shit,*" I mutter as I lean back in my seat. "When did you read that?"

"Late last night. All night," he chuckles. "Damn, bro, you are one horny dude, huh? Putting all that online about your wife is pretty hot, though."

"It wasn't about her," I tell him. "The character is Sophia and I didn't mean to send it out the way that I did anyway. I've deleted it all as of this morning."

"Doesn't matter," Todd informs me. "They know."

"Who?" My friend points up to the ceiling. Suddenly, I realize that management has seen the email as well as the link I sent out.

"Shit."

"No, no, don't worry about it. I've talked them out of anything rash. I convinced them that I already knew about the whole thing and that we've had a conversation. Your email was hacked, right? At least, that has to be what happened. Someone wanted to embarrass you and get some clicks to an adult forum where someone with a name similar to Sophie's was being written about. You're cool with them, Ollie All is well."

"I'm not fired?"

"Nope. You're welcome."

"Shit," I say again. "That wasn't supposed to go out to all those people, Todd. I was trying to just blow off a little steam with those stories and then get some feedback. Sophie doesn't really do any of those things."

A disappointed look crosses my friend's face. "She doesn't? Damn, man. I was having wet dreams all night about her." He laughs as he crosses his arms. "Does she know about your little pastime?"

My face turns deep red. "She does now. Sophie was one of the ones I sent the link to accidentally yesterday afternoon. Honestly, I have probably cut my own dick off this time. Things don't look good between us."

"Pissed her off?" I nod my head. "I thought Sophie was more adventurous, though?"

"You know better," I chuckle. "We've talked about the things that I can't get her to do. My wife hates some of the things I have written about, especially including the ones of her with other men. She made me sleep on the sofa last night."

Todd shakes his head. "You've stepped in it, Ollie. What are you going to do about it now that she knows?"

I sigh. "Well, I just finished deleting everything. It's all gone now and hopefully that will limit the number of people who have access to it. That's going to disappoint my subscribers, but..."

"Whoa, man, you have subscribers for that shit?" Todd laughs. "I'll bet that was getting you a boner once in a while, huh?" As he continues to laugh, I can't help but allow a grin to cross my own face.

"I had subscribers, yeah, but now that's all gone. Nothing was a paid thing, though. It was all for fun. Sophie, though, doesn't see the fun in it all. It's gone now, so hopefully the damage I have done will be minimal."

Todd nods his head. "I've already downloaded copies of everything, so that's good with me."

"Oh, come on," I laugh. "You actually kept copies?"

"That's some good writing, Ollie. You should be proud of the way you put those stories together. Honestly, your wife should be happy with them too."

I shrug my shoulders. "She thinks that they are nasty and disgusting. I wouldn't be surprised if I hear today that Sophie has an attorney and is getting ready to draw up the papers for a divorce. She was pretty pissed off last night."

"She's not going to divorce you, dude," he tells me. "You fucked up by letting her find out about your little literary adventure, but Sophie loves you. Even I can see that whenever I see her hop up here to see you on her lunch break. I can't think of any other wife around here who would do that for her husband."

Todd is right. Sophie has been a wonderful partner in life for me. She will come to my workplace about once a week and we will go out for lunch nearby. Her shop is only two blocks away, so it has been somewhat of a tradition for us. That is something that is likely all in the past now. I cannot see her doing that now that I have betrayed her by writing about fantasies that include her online.

"I don't know. She's angrier than I've ever seen her before. We have had a few arguments over the years, but I think this one has gone way over the top for her. She didn't even kiss me goodbye this morning as she left for work."

Todd smiles. "She'll come around, man. They always do." He shifts around in his seat and asks, "So, are those stories just fantasies of *yours?* Things that you want to do with her but can't?"

"Yeah, I guess you can say that. Fantasies. I would love our love life to be a little more on fire, but Sophie just isn't that sort of woman. She doesn't like thinking about that sort of thing. I guess I can't blame her, though. I mean, I do sometimes really push the whole narrative about her screwing around while I watch. There have been times when I have even caught myself wishing that she would cheat on me and then tell me all about it later."

"Have you tried to get something like that going with her? Maybe if she saw what you really wanted, Sophie would be agreeable to something? Even if it was just some heavy petting?"

I laugh. "I can see it in your eyes already, Todd. No, she isn't going to let you fondle her and she's not going to give you a blow job."

He laughs along with me. "I'm serious, though. Take me out of the equation. Are there times when it seems that your wife is maybe a little bit willing to go along with the fantasy? Maybe she has said something during sex?"

I think for a moment. "Maybe once or twice. Sophie generally hates talking about something like that, even during sex. I was lucky to get her to let me fuck her on the beach a couple of weeks ago."

"What?" My friend seems to perk up as he looks back at me. "Was this on a *public* beach? Around other people?" I can tell by the look on Todd's face that he is very interested in what I have just mentioned to him.

"Easy, man. It was a public beach, but I was very careful. You probably wouldn't have noticed what was going on even if you were ten feet away."

Todd's face contorts as he shakes his head. "Was it really *sex,* then? No wonder you two are having issues. Shit, Ollie, sex should be something that a person could pick out fifty feet away. What did you do, just slide your dick into her while lying on the sand?"

"Um, well..."

"*Fuck.* She isn't into your fantasies because you're a bore in bed, buddy. You have to spice things up enough to get Sophie to want to take things further. Screwing her secretly like that is just a wet dream gone wrong." He laughs at his own comment, but can quickly see that I'm not amused in the same way. "Sorry, Ollie. Look, I think she might be convinced with a little planning, but that's up to you to do it. Just show your wife how much you want to live out some of your fantasies. Do it in a loving way and I'm sure she will respond positively to you. She has to."

"Sophie isn't like other women, Todd."

"Treat her like other women and she will be," he pushes. "Stop letting her get away with her prudish behavior. Tell her that you are the man and you want to see her play with other guys. Even if it's just the little stuff, it's better than nothing at all. You have to assert yourself, man. Push for what you want. Don't let her dominate how sex will go between the two of you." Though Todd is often a jokester about this topic, it's fairly obvious at this point that he is being perfectly serious. His suggestion comes from genuine concern opposed to the sexual remarks he often utters.

I nod my head. "You might have something there. I'll have to have a serious discussion with her, but until then I need to just fix the shit I've already spread throughout our marriage. Are you sure that management is okay with what has happened in the whole email thing?"

"Like I told you, I have explained to them that it wasn't really your fault. Someone hacked your account and we have fixed the problem. I even have an IT guy who will vouch for you."

"I thought you said that I had gotten past the IT department, unlike Steve."

"I didn't say that *exactly*," he replies. "This guy, he has typed up a memo about viruses in emails and how to avoid them. You'll look like a moron for opening up an email you shouldn't have, but no one will be any the wiser. You're cool, dude. Just keep me up on what happens with the wife." Todd stands to his feet and walks to the door. Turning, he adds, "Have a good day, Ollie. I know things are tough right now, but it will all get better soon. Just wait and see." He turns and leaves my office before closing the door behind him.

"Wow," I chuckle quietly while running my hands over the top of my desk. "Thank goodness Todd covered for me with management. If only I could do that when it comes to my wife." I sigh as I turn to my computer to check my emails. True to Todd's promise, an IT department email is waiting there for all employees. It concerns the use of email and how to avoid a hacker's attempts to get to our information. Sure, it is a little embarrassing as a lot of people here got my email last night and know the IT email is about me, but it is certainly worth saving my job. Now if only I can save my marriage.

Chapter Six: A Deep Conversation

It takes some convincing through text messages, but Sophie eventually agrees to meet me at a restaurant for lunch. As we sit down, I notice that she does not look directly at me with her blue eyes. This is so different from what she normally does that I feel I must say something.

"You're really upset with me, aren't you? You hate me now."

Sophie sighs and then looks at me. "Ollie, I am having a hard time getting past what you wrote about me on that website. The things you claimed that I am doing aren't true at all, but there are those who think now that they are. How do you fix that kind of thing? You really can't." She fumbles with her cell phone as a young male server comes to our table.

"Can I get you something to drink?"

"A cup of coffee, please. The sugar and creamer on the side, please."

The man then turns to me. "And you, sir?"

I look up at him and think about how attractive he is. The server is the sort of guy I would love to see Sophie in bed with while I watch. It is a terrible thing to think while I am already in trouble with her over my fantasies. "I'll take a glass of water with some lemon."

"Right away." He smiles at the two of us and then walks away.

My wife sits back in her seat as she puts the menu down on the table. "I'm not really all that hungry."

"I'm sorry," I reply as I realize her lack of appetite is likely tied to what I have done. "Maybe we can share an appetizer?" Sophie nods her head slightly and I look on the menu for something that I know we will both like.

"I saw that the posts are now gone," she notes quietly as she fidgets in her seat. "At least that's a little less of a problem to deal with now."

"Very few actually saw them, honey. I was told by the IT department that the email was only opened by a handful of people at work before they blocked the link. You won't be hearing from anyone from there."

"They *know?*" Sophie's face turns red. "The IT department at your workplace knows about the stories that you wrote about me?"

"They think it was a hacker that put those links in an email," I try to explain as I smile slightly. "Honey, it's all taken care of. The damage is minimal and you don't have to worry about anything. If your brother does open the email, it will come back as no account on the site. I've deleted everything."

"Good."

"Here you go." The server returns with our drinks and places them on the table in front of us. "Are you ready to order?"

"Just an appetizer," I reply. "How about the loaded potato skins? You like those, right?" I say as I look at Sophie. She nods her head. "That's all for now. We might want something more later, but just bring us those and some of that ranch dip you make here."

"As you wish." The young man smiles before taking the menus from our hands. As he walks away, I can see that my wife is thinking about something. "What is it, honey? Be honest with me, alright? You're not going to upset me. Now is the time for us to try to work things out between us."

Sophie puts some sugar and creamer in her coffee before taking a sip and cradling the warm cup in her hands. "There is a good reason that I don't like even talking about your fantasies, Ollie. There's something about me that you don't know. Something that I have tried to put way behind me over the last few years."

"Like what?" I say with interest as I take a sip of my water. Sophie again fidgets in her seat. Whatever it is that she is about to share is likely a big deal to her, no matter how small it might seem to me.

"You and I met after college," she begins as she looks across the table at me. "We didn't know each other while there, and so there are things that we haven't talked about."

"Like boyfriends, girlfriends, and things like that," I reply. "You and I agreed that we would just leave that chapter of our lives on the shelf and not discuss whatever happened. It seemed to be the best thing for us when we made that agreement."

"I think that in order for you to understand my position on everything, I need to open that part of my life up to you just a little. You see, I had a boyfriend my junior year of college named Marcus."

"Marcus. Okay. What about him?" I am not at all the jealous type, but something about this former boyfriend already bothers me. Maybe he was the one right before me? Could it be that she was going to marry him at one time?"

"Yeah, Marcus. You see, we were together for about nine months until something happened at a party one night." Sophie takes another quick sip of her hot coffee. Whatever it is that she wants to share with me is obviously too difficult to simply spit out all at once. After some thought, she continues, "We were invited to a joint fraternity and sorority party off-campus. There was a lot of alcohol there, and some light drugs like pot, but I was pretty good at first. Marcus encouraged me to loosen up a little by taking some shots of tequila, and that's where things began to change for me."

"What changed?" I ask.

"Me," she replies while looking into my eyes. "I changed, Ollie. I went from being a nice girl to someone that I just didn't recognize. Things got weird that night."

"Weird? In what way?" My interest is piqued now that Sophie is opening up to me about her past college life.

My wife seems to temper her words as she responds, "Marcus and I began to make out on the couch in the living room. There were others there doing the same thing too, so I thought very little of it as I gave in to what was happening. Then..." Her voice trails off as she thinks for a moment. "I don't know how it happened, but Marcus and I ended up naked on that couch and he had my legs back while screwing me. There were about twenty or thirty other college students there watching and taking pictures while this all happened. Marcus came inside me with no condom, and I then sucked one of his friend's dicks for him. I'm not sure what else happened because I only saw those pictures after the party later that week." Her face red, Sophie looks down at her hands on the table. "Those pictures were shared all over the campus and even through other forms of email and social media, Ollie. It was embarrassing and I broke things off with Marcus soon after that."

"Shit." I sit quietly as I let what my wife has told me to sink in. "You did all that while people were watching?" She nods her head slowly while looking around the small restaurant. It is apparent that Sophie is not proud of what happened that night at the party, but now I can see why she doesn't like my little fantasies.

"Here you are," the server says as he walks up and places a large dish between the two of us. He then puts a small plate for each of us down and asks, "Can I get you anything else right now?"

"No, thank you," I reply as I look up at him.

"Enjoy." The young man walks away and I turn my attention back to Sophie.

"I can see why you are so upset with me now. I'm so sorry, honey."

"Oliver, things sometimes bother me when they really shouldn't. I understand why you want a wife who would do those things, but then I worry about what would be said about me if people found out that I was doing what you wanted me to do."

"Wait," I say as I realize something. "You have *thought* about this, haven't you?"

She nods her head. "I've considered letting you have your way with those fantasies. I'm just too worried about what might happen, though. You can understand that, can't you?"

My heart beats quickly as I think about the small window of opportunity that has appeared during our conversation. "I understand. But, are you saying that you might be willing to do something sexual with another man if I could keep it completely quiet?"

"Ollie..."

"Honey, please. Just tell me. Do you have some of the same fantasies I do? Would you like to try something with another man?" My cock hardens as I think about the answer that might come from her.

After some quiet thought, she tells me, "I don't know. Maybe. I would have to know that there was no way that we would be discovered doing that."

I swallow hard as my excitement becomes difficult to hide. "Todd Dunigan."

She frowns. "What about him?"

"I know you aren't all that into him, but he saw the short stories I posted online and he would like to talk to you about them."

"Oliver. What have you done?"

"He's not married and he's about as secretive as a guy can be, Sophie. He would make a perfect choice for a fantasy like this. He also would die before telling other people about anything I ask him to keep secret."

"Todd." My wife's face turns a little pink as she considers him. There is some difficult history between the two of them, so bringing up his name is only an attempt on my part to try to move this topic forward. I have no idea who else I could offer to Sophie so quickly.

"He says he loves the way you look. He asks about you all the time and he has told me that the biggest fantasy he has involves you. I know that you don't like him much, but he really is a good guy, honey. If you would be willing to consider him, I think it would work out well for all of us."

Sophie looks at me and then reaches for a potato skin. She dips it into some ranch sauce and then bites into it, her mind obviously racing with thoughts. Have I stumbled upon something that I could convince my wife to do? Is this really happening?

"I don't know," she finally says. "After what happened in college, I'm a little worried about that sort of thing, Ollie. It's not something that I ever want to happen to me again."

"The pictures?" She nods her head. "There won't be any pictures taken if you do this. I promise. We can meet in neutral territory to make sure of that. Todd would be really happy to be a part of this too."

"Maybe." There it is again! That word! It seems that my wife is slowly coming around to my way of thinking. "You wouldn't think less of me if that happened?"

I shake my head. "No, never! I would love it, honey." I reach for a potato skin as well and after dunking it into the ranch sauce take a taste of it. "This is really good."

"Yeah, I like these." Sophie reaches for another one. This is a good sign as I begin to see her whole attitude on sex with other men begin to change. How far she is willing to go, though, is still to be seen.

"So, sex with Todd?"

"*Sex?*" She swallows a bit of the potato skin. "Maybe. I don't know, Oliver, this is all just going so quickly. There are a whole lot of concerns that I have about doing something like this."

"I know. But, if we work together on this, we can get rid of some of those concerns. We make a great couple, Sophie. You and I can do this and have a great time at it. We don't have to be afraid of sex with friends."

My wife nods her head. "I'll think about it, alright? Just give me a little time."

"How is everything?" the server asks as he steps back to our table. I jump in my seat a little as I did not expect to see him back so quickly.

"It's very nice," Sophie answers. "What is the lunch special today?"

"Ah, it's chef salad with a side of breadsticks."

"I'll have that," she tells him. "What about you, Ollie?"

I smile as I raise an eyebrow. "I suppose I'll have the same." I nod my head at the server and watch as he walks away. "And?"

"We'll talk later," Sophie tells me. "Let's just enjoy our lunch for now."

Sign up to my Patreon account and receive exclusive Hotwife stories every month and sexy scenes every week!

https://www.patreon.com/karlyviolet

Chapter Seven: Resounding Ovation

"It's back up," Todd tells me as he walks into my office with his cell phone. He shows me the screen and I almost vomit as I realize that my entire forum account is back up with all of the stories I have written.

"What the *fuck?*" I grumble as I take the cell phone from him and scroll through the stories.

"I'm willing to bet that you would have to contact the administrator of the website personally to delete everything, Ollie. It appears that your stories are a solid hit with subscribers and they don't want to lose them. I'm sure the site is making money from them."

"Fuck." I see a smirk on my friend's face and shake my head. "This isn't funny. If Sophie sees this, I'm dead."

"You'll survive," he responds. "It's not the end of the world. You just didn't go through all of the channels to get everything pulled down." Todd takes back his phone and points to something on the screen. "More than a thousand people have read the latest post, Ollie. It has a solid five-star review, too. I wouldn't take it down, just see if you can get a cut of whatever money they are making off your stories."

"She's going to flip out," I mutter as I shake my head.

"Come on, man, you're a star on this website. They love you. Look at the comments." Todd scrolls to the comments below my post. "This guy loves the way your wife gives head in your story. Oh, and here's one who wants to have Sophie put on a strap-on and give it to him from behind." He laughs as he continues to scroll. "Some of these dudes want to meet Sophie and have sex with her while you watch, Ollie. You've got to think this through before trying to get rid of the entire account again."

I shudder as I think about my wife. "She'll see them. I know she will."

"But, you told me in a text last night that things looked better for the two of you. You told me that Sophie is thinking about doing something like what you want." Though I shared that much with my colleague, I have not yet told him that his name came up several times during that conversation with my wife. I do not want to spill those beans until I have something more firm with what Sophie is willing to do and not to do.

"There's a lot for me to process here. Why would they put my shit back up after I deleted the account?"

"Money, man. It's all about the money. There's probably some fine print agreement that you agreed to that gives them the right to do this. You probably clicked through it when you made your account in the beginning. Your stories are drawing lots of traffic to the website."

"It's probably all about money," I admit.

"What did the two of you say to each other? I know you told me some of it already, but what else was said? Do you want to tell me that?" Todd has a seat in front of my desk and smiles as he crosses his arms over his chest.

I sigh. "A name came up while we talked about what Sophie might be willing to do. It's a name that I haven't yet looked into for certain."

"A name? Like a *lucky guy?* Who is he, Ollie? Come on, man, don't leave me hanging for long." He leans forward and looks at me from across my desk. It only takes a momentary glance for him to have his answer. "Fuck, yes! *Yes!*" He stands up from his chair and raises his arms into the air. "You mentioned me to her, didn't you? Was she okay with that idea or is she still a little pissed at me over that party thing?"

"The party thing is still a problem for her," I tell him. "Sophie doesn't just forgive and forget for some things, Todd. You were a real shit that day."

"But, she's *thinking* about it, isn't she? *Fuck yeah!*" He smiles from ear to ear while sitting back down in the chair. "So, will this happen soon, or what?"

I laugh as I shake my head. "I don't know. This whole thing with the website could scare her away again. There are some things that I only recently found out as to why Sophie has been so resistant to my fantasies. So, that being said, we will have to wait and see what she decides."

"Invite me over to your house, Ollie. I know that I can convince her if I am there. I'm great with women." The smile on his face seems to continue to grow as he considers sex with my wife. I am not certain that this is the sort of thing that makes me happy, to be honest.

"To my house? *Dinner?*" I shrug my shoulders. "I guess it might be worth a try to ask her."

"It's a great idea," he tells me. "She will love me by the time dinner is over."

"Down boy," I say with a chuckle. "Sophie might just hate you even more afterwards. You can't be certain that things will really go your way."

"Maybe." He stands to his feet. "I've got to get out of here and have a drink. Want to go across the street with me?"

"It's eleven in the morning," I chuckle. "We are at work. You can't just go have a drink at the bar."

"Sure I can." Todd smiles at me. "I know the human resources manager personally." He winks at me before turning and leaving my office. For my part, I sit back in my seat and think for a moment about what I now know.

My cell phone buzzes on my desk and I pick it up. A text message from my wife has arrived, so I open it up and shake my head. "They're all back up," she begins.

I think about what I can say to her to blunt the news. "I'm sorry, honey. Really I am." I can't think of how else to respond as I get another message ready for her. "Honestly, I had nothing to do with it. I think the forum admin put it back up. I'll try to get it all back down today."

"Wait," she replies. I sit motionless for a moment as I try to understand what she means by waiting. "Have you read the comments?"

I swallow hard. "Yeah, I've seen some of them. Sorry, baby."

"No, have you read them all? Some of them are pretty cool." Goosebumps rise along my arms as I read her message to me. Is Sophie telling me that she's okay with having the stories online now? What has suddenly changed?

"I've read a few of them. Do you like some of them?"

"Maybe." A smiley face appears in this text message from my wife. I feel my cock becoming hard as I think about how this is turning out for us. Something has changed in Sophie's thinking as she has been reading the stories and the fan comments that go along with them. "You're popular on this forum, Ollie. Very popular."

"I just had that same conversation with Todd," I quip before I realize what I have texted to her.

"Um, did you tell him?" she asks.

"He already knows about the forum thread, honey." My hands shake as I send this message to my wife.

"No, about what we talked about. About you saying that he wants to do those sorts of things with me?"

I think for a moment before I respond. Is this a test? Is my wife simply setting me up to have a reason for divorce? Text messages are admissible as evidence in such cases. At least, that's what I have read online recently. Parsing my words, I ask, "Would that upset you if I had?"

It takes a moment, but her response comes back. "I've been doing a lot of thinking this morning, Ollie. Maybe I could do this? Maybe with Todd? I don't know." She puts an emoji in the text message that has its hands up as if shrugging.

My cock leaks some pre-come into my pants as I consider what this could mean for us. If my wife is telling me that she might be willing to fuck Todd while I watch, it is the culmination of sexual desire for me in the fantasies that I have hoped would be fulfilled. Still, I worry that she might be baiting me into something, so I wait for a moment before replying.

"Todd would like to come to dinner tonight with us just to talk," I text back. "Just to talk, alright?"

"To talk? Tonight?" I get the feeling that I might have crossed a line here by being so bold, but I want to see if this is something that Sophie is truly getting into.

"Dinner and talking. That's all. He wants to talk with the two of us. He's a nice guy, honey. I think it would be a nice dinner."

"Dinner," she replies in a text message. "Just dinner. Nothing else?"

"Nothing else," I assure her. "Just talking and eating. We don't even have to mention all the stories I have written or anything else that has been going on. That's Todd's suggestion." I lie, but I feel that I might need to do so to close the deal for dinner among the three of us at our house.

There is no return message for a moment and I begin to worry. Sophie could be plotting her next move to get me into divorce court. After all, I have practically laid all of my cards out before her. It would be an easy case to argue that I have been pushing her to fuck other men against her wishes.

"Dinner is fine," she soon texts back. "Can you pick something up for dinner? Maybe Chinese or Thai?"

I smile as I answer. "Yes, I can do that. I'll get some wine too."

"No wine," Sophie answers. "No alcohol at all. I don't want to do anything that I don't know that I'm doing. We will enjoy some food and whatever else we have to drink. Okay?" A smiling emoji pops up after this text message to me.

"Sounds good. I'll let him know." I send a smiling emoji back and then hear nothing else from her at this point. Putting my cell phone back down on my desk, I sit back in my chair and consider what this all means.

"Holy shit, Ollie. You have really done it, haven't you? Not only did your stories get put back up, but now Sophie wants to see Todd at dinner in your own home. What if she wants to have sex with him tonight?" I realize there is very little chance of this, but who knows? My wife has changed her mind so dramatically that it has shocked me this morning. Now I will need to get Todd back in here to tell him that he will be dining at my house tonight. My only hope is that he shows up and is completely respectful to Sophie. She will likely not put up with any of his shenanigans while eating dinner with us. This will simply be a time to feel each other out. I am sure my wife is just as eager to figure things out as I am, so we will simply enjoy dinner together tonight. Nothing else.

Chapter Eight: Resistance is Futile

Sophie and I have decided to order a meal from a local Chinese restaurant. We expect the meal to be delivered soon as we answer the door and see Todd standing on the other side.

"Hey, I hope I'm not too early," he says as he walks in. I close the door behind him and watch as he smiles and nods at my wife. "Good to see you again, Sophie."

She smiles sheepishly before replying, "Yeah, it's good to see you too, Todd." There is a certain amount of tension in the room as the two of them walk up and take each other's hands. Todd pulls her hand to his mouth and kisses it softly, which is the sort of thing I had hoped that he would just stay away from tonight. However, my wife seems to accept the offer of affection before we go to the dining room for some non-alcoholic drinks.

"It's apple cider," I tell my friend. "No alcohol, though."

"Oh. It's good." He takes a second sip of it after having a strange look on his face right after having his first sip.

"I'm sorry, that was my request," Sophie tells him. "It's just something that I prefer to do when I have dinner with guests."

"Not a problem," Todd replies. "I'm cool with that." He smiles at the two of us as he looks around. "And what about dinner?"

"Chinese," I answer. Looking at my phone, I add, "Three minutes and it will be here. Just have a seat." Todd and I wait for my wife to sit down before we have a seat as well. The cider is cool, not hot as it would normally be when consumed. However, it's actually very good. The recipe for the cider came from an online food forum that my wife visits occasionally. We considered getting grape juice or something else that would be more like wine, but we finally settled on the apple cider instead.

"I like Chinese. Did you get any of those fortune cookies?"

I nod my head. "I think it comes with something like six of them." The conversation is leading nowhere as we sit and look at each other. I can understand why Sophie is quiet, but it is a rare thing indeed to see my friend from work so quiet and reserved.

"So, you are the HR manager at your company, right?" Sophie finally says to our guest. "I'll bet that's interesting."

Todd nods his head. "It can have it's ups and downs," he replies. "We had to fire a woman for stealing office supplies a couple of weeks ago. I suppose that was a bit of a downer for some there."

"But not for you," my wife notes. "You don't seem to be so torn up over it."

"Nah, not really," he admits. "She was stealing, so I really didn't mind wielding the firing hammer for that. The lady got what she deserved."

"I see." Sophie's eyes turn to me for a moment just as the doorbell rings.

"The food is here," I say as I get up and go to get the delivery. As I get to the door and accept the Chinese food delivery, I can hear the two of them continue to talk. The thought of the two of them having such a cordial conversation was one that I would not have heard just a week or so ago.

"Thank you," the delivery driver says after I hand her a tip. I close the door and carry the two bags of Chinese food to the dining room table.

"It's hot," I tell them as I put the bags on the table. "Be careful." We pull out boxes of rice as well as orange chicken and beef lo mein. As promised, there are fortune cookies, only it appears that there are several more than I had expected. Todd is quick to take one of them from the table and open the package.

"I always like to know how things will turn out during dinner, so I open a cookie to see what I can expect."

Sophie chuckles. "Do you really do that?"

He nods his head. "Absolutely. I mean, there's a lot of wisdom in one little cookie." Todd smiles as he opens the cookie and pulls the small slip of paper from within. "Dreams will come true for you soon. Keep trying." There is a silence that permeates the dining room as we all mull what he has read from the small slip of paper.

"Well, that's interesting," I finally say as I hand everyone a small plate that has come with the meal. I sit down and we begin to divide the food between us.

After eating for a couple of minutes with nothing said between us, Todd asks, "Do the two of you eat this way often?"

"Chinese?"

"Take out or delivery," he replies.

I nod my head. "Only whenever the mood strikes us or we feel like being a little lazy. I'm a pretty good cook, though, so I normally make dinner for the two of us."

"Excuse me?" Sophie laughs as she finishes off a small bite of orange chicken. "I cook just as much as you do, Ollie."

I raise an eyebrow and smile. "Do you really call that cooking?" Todd and I laugh as it appears that my wife has taken great offense to the comment. It is not long before she begins to laugh as well.

"Maybe my meals aren't the sort of meals you like to cook, but they are completely edible and pretty damned tasty."

"Grilled cheese," I lament while grinning at my friend beside me. "She calls grilled cheese sandwiches a meal."

"They have basil and a touch of romano cheese in them too, Oliver. Come on, you know that they are really good. I even use sourdough bread for them."

I smile as I lean back in my seat. "Well, I do have to admit they are pretty tasty. Still, there really isn't much preparation needed to make that sort of thing. It's hard to consider it a serious meal unless you put some real effort into it."

"Fuck you," she laughs while shaking her head.

"Whoa, language," Todd jokes.

Sophie turns and looks at him. "So, tell me what you think is going to happen between us tonight." The sudden comment throws me off as it does Todd as well. He looks at me briefly before turning to look at my wife.

"Well, I don't know. I thought we would just enjoy a nice dinner. I don't mean to be intrusive..."

"You *are* intrusive," Sophie tells him. "You know what you want and I know what you want. I guess I'm just curious how far you think this is going to go." My wife's sudden change in demeanor seems curious as I begin to pray that Todd just plays things cool. This could be, after all, some sort of test she has decided to put to him.

My colleague puts down his chopsticks and nods his head. "Fair enough. I think Ollie has probably told you that I wouldn't mind being the other guy, right?" Sophie nods her head slightly. "Well, I wanted to have dinner with you to see if there is any chemistry. Like I started to say earlier, I don't mean to be intrusive, but I think there is something between us. I feel it, and I think that you do too."

My wife's face turns red. "I don't think I feel it, Todd. Honestly, I still have a hard time getting over how crude you were at that party."

"Crude? It was just a joke."

"You commented on my pantyline through my pants and I didn't even know you yet," Sophie retorts. "You asked me if I had tan lines or if I laid out naked. Don't you think that was just a little too much for a guy to ask a woman he barely knew?" She shakes her head and adds, "And the thing about my mother. Who are you to bring that up to me?"

My heart races as I watch the looks that transpire between them. Todd gets up from his seat and walks over to my wife. After looking down at her for a moment, he bends down and presses his lips to hers. Though I expect Sophie to resist, she does not. Instead, she stands up and they embrace fully, their bodies pulling close together as they run their hands over each other.

"Fuck," I say quietly as I adjust the boner I am getting inside my pants. "Holy fuck."

Todd's hand moves into my wife's tee shirt as he searches for one of her bra-covered C-cup orbs. He finds one and gently squeezes it as her hand finds his crotch. The hardon he has is apparent as she gently tugs at it. Pre-coming in my own pants, I begin to hope that they will soon be undressed and fucking each other at the dinner table.

"No," Sophie suddenly says as she pulls away. My friend's hand drops out of her shirt. "This isn't the way it's going to be. You can't just come in here and take me." My wife looks sharply at me before turning and going to our bedroom. The door closes and I hear the lock turn before Todd sits back down in his seat.

"She wants me," he says quietly.

"Yeah, sure she does. It's why Sophie just marched out of here."

"No, really. I could feel it. She really wants to do it, Ollie. There's just too much holding her back, though." He looks at me and says, "There's stuff you haven't told me, huh? Something happened to her that involved alcohol. That's why Sophie didn't want it here tonight."

"She just doesn't like alcohol," I reply.

"Bullshit. I've seen you have drinks with her. *Alcoholic* drinks. There's something else to all of this. Spill it."

Leaning forward on my elbows on the table, I quietly say, "There was an incident at a party she went to in college where she very publicly had sex with a guy after she got drunk. Sophie doesn't want to have sex with alcohol inside her now so that she can better control what happens."

"Oh." Todd nods his head. "I get that and I can respect it, man. Still, she wants me. Her hands were all over me and she was even tugging at the little man."

"The *little man?*" I chuckle.

"He's my wingman. My compadre. *Mi amigo.*"

"Fuck." We both laugh. I turn my head and look at the bedroom door where my wife is hiding out. "She won't come out while you're still here."

"I figured as much. We need to do this again, though. She's close." Todd reaches for the orange chicken box and stands to his feet. "Thanks for the meal, man."

"You're taking the whole box?"

He grins and replies, "You won't eat it all anyway, right? Besides, you have a wife to deal with and I have hunger issues."

"Hunger issues." We both laugh as I stand up and see him to the door. Soon, Todd is gone and I am left alone with a Chinese meal and a wife who has suddenly become nervous of the situation. "Alright?" I ask through the bedroom door.

There is no response at first, but eventually she answers, "Just let me be by myself for a while, okay? You can sleep in here tonight, but give me an hour to just get over that."

"Anything for you, baby." I leave the doorway to put away the leftover food in the refrigerator. Sophie doesn't seem to be upset. Instead, she seems confused and in need of straightening things out in her own mind. I will give her the time she needs. She deserves at least that much.

Chapter Nine: Surprise Visit

62

Sophie eventually came out of our bedroom last night, but very little was said between us about dinner and what happened with Todd. She did not seem too upset about the rounding to second base with Todd Dunigan, but I do get the feeling that it was not what she had really expected to happen during dinner. As a matter of fact, it caught me completely off-guard as well.

"Good morning, Rachel," I say to the young receptionist as I walk into the company's building.

"Morning, Oliver. Did you sleep well?"

"Uh, more or less," I say with a smile. It is the sort of small talk I have had with Rachel over the last year or so since she was hired for her current position. Making my way to my office, I think about what to say to Todd today. I am certain he will be by eventually to hash out the evening's events.

I close the door of my office and make my way to my desk. Just as I sit down, I hear my office door open. "Todd, let me at least have my coffee, buddy."

"It's not Todd." I turn to see Sophie closing the door behind her. She walks up to my desk and stands right in front of me. "I'm sorry, I know I shouldn't be here right now, but there is a lot that we need to talk about, Ollie."

"Honey, aren't you supposed to be at the shop?"

"I took the morning off," she tells me. "I'm still just a little bothered by last night and my employees have things handled."

Sighing, I wave toward the seat in front of my desk. My wife sits down and I do the same on the other side. "I'm really sorry about the way he came at you, Sophie. I plan to have a talk with Todd this morning. As a matter of fact, I thought you were him just now."

"Yeah, I noticed," she answers. "I think he and I both got into what happened last night, so I'm not really blaming him for anything. It just all went so fast that I was a little surprised."

Nodding, I reply, "It shocked me a little too, but I was getting into it myself." I chuckle as goosebumps rise along my neck. I begin to wonder whether that was the right thing to say. "Like I said, I'll tell him that what happened last night should have probably waited until you were ready."

Sophie smiles softly. "I think I was ready, but that scared me a little. So, I ran."

"Ready?"

"Yeah, ready. He's an attractive guy, even if he can be a sort of asshole sometimes, Ollie. He kisses really nicely too."

My jaw drops a little. "Are you saying that you *want* to have sex with him?"

"I don't know." Sophie looks at my desk phone and nods her head. "Why don't you call him into your office so that he can be in on this conversation. I feel like we all need to be here."

"Oh. Okay." I lift the receiver on my desk phone and ring Todd's office. "Hey, are you busy? Would you mind coming by real quick? Thanks." I hang up the phone and look over at Sophie. "He's on his way."

"Great." She smiles at me nervously as I try to guess what she might say to him. My wife has admitted to me that she wants to have a little fun with him in bed, but will she go as far as to say that to Todd?"

My office door opens just moments later. "Hey, man..." He stops as his eyes settle upon my wife.

"Just close the door and come here," I say as I wave him over. Todd does as I ask and makes his way to the desk. As he does, Sophie stands to her feet and turns to greet him. Only, I do not expect the greeting she then gives him.

"Just be quiet," she tells him as she kneels in front of him and reaches for his pants. My wife makes quick work of opening his zipper and feeling around inside to find his quickly erecting cock. Todd's manhood is inside Sophie's mouth before it is completely hard.

"*Shit,*" he mutters as she begins to suck hard on him. Her small, soft hand moves into his pants again and finds his large balls. She pulls them out and moves down to nibble on them as his body quakes just three feet from my desk.

"Sophie..." I cannot believe what I am seeing as she pleasures my friend orally.

"Motherfucker," Todd moans as he enjoys the feeling of my wife's soft, wet mouth wrapped around his johnson. Sophie is an oral perfectionist when it comes to sucking cock. I think she felt that it was her responsibility to become so good when she decided to refuse my fantasies. It is her way of making certain that she keeps me completely happy.

"*Utt...*" Sophie gags herself on his long shaft a little, almost all of his eight inches or so buried deep inside my wife's throat. I get hard as I watch and soon I pull my own cock out of my pants so that I can play with myself behind my desk.

"Oh, baby," Todd says as he runs his fingers through her hair. She sucks and slurps along his entire length as he closes his eyes and just enjoys the moment. Sophie seems happy to be doing this for my colleague as she reaches into her own blouse and begins to play with her nipples.

"Here." I push my cock back into my pants and reach out across my desk. I push everything into the floor and offer them a place close to me to have their fun. Sophie gets up and smiles as she begins to remove her blouse. Todd helps her with her bra, a light blue number that I bought her about a year ago. Her C-cup breasts soon pop out as he unclasps the back strap and I watch as he goes down to suck on one of her large, pink nipples. Sophie throws her head back and moans as she runs her fingers through his dark hair.

"*Fuck,*" my wife moans as her skirt drops and Todd's fingers find her wet slit. He inserts a finger and begins to play with her moist tunnel, my cock stiffening as I imagine what it is like for him to feel her softness. "Oh, fuck, Todd." My friend helps her onto the desk and then Sophie lays back. He pushes her legs back and presses his face into her smoothly waxed clapper. "Holy shit."

"That's it," I say as I reach out and run a hand over my wife's taut nipple. She's horny and ready for her new lover as he pushes her legs back and runs his tongue over her wet snapper. "How does she taste?"

Todd turns to look at me, a little bit of my wife's wetness on his face. "She's sweet, man. Really sweet." He goes back down on her, causing Sophie's feet to point hard, her toes flexed as if she is a ballerina ready to spin.

"Oh, shit. Fuck. I might come." Sophie's face is red as her body shakes from the intense pleasure Todd is giving her orally. "Holy fuck, I really might come."

"Wait, okay?" He stands up and pulls off his shirt before sliding his pants down. Once his briefs are down to his feet, my friend strokes his long cock a couple of times before pressing the head of it against my wife's hard clit. He rubs it along her crease as she bucks around on the desk in front of me. Then, as if by some magic, the long, meaty phallus disappears into her hole.

"Fuck, you're so big," she moans as her body shakes. Todd begins to thrust in and out of her, his balls bouncing off her puckered asshole.

"You're so *tight*," he groans as he enjoys her soft *muff*. "Sophie you are such a hot little bitch." Although I know my friend to have a crass vocabulary, I find myself surprised that he would call Sophie a bitch. He lifts her ass from the desk and pulls her hard to himself. *"Fuck."*

"AHHHH!!!" Sophie winces a little. "You're deep," she tells him. *"Fucking deep."* Todd ignores her as he plows deep into her birth canal. *"Ohhh...owww..."* It doesn't take long for her to begin to enjoy each thrust, though, as he reaches down and plays with her swollen clitoris.

"I can't believe I'm fucking you," Todd says as he works around inside her pussy. "Sophie, thank you for letting me do this."

"Thank you," she giggles as she begins to grind into him. My wife's sweet pelvis twists and turns as Todd has his way with her. He finds her G-spot and soon she gives way to a powerful orgamsm. *"FUCK!"*

"Not so loud," I plead as I look over at my office door. Though I hoped that it would be locked, it is not.

"Uhhhh!!!" Sophie squeaks loudly enough that I wonder who might be able to hear her. Though the walls to my office are fairly well insulated, there is no guarantee that they are insulated enough. *"Todd..."*

"OHHHH!!! Uhhh...mmmmm...uhhh..." His penis suddenly explodes inside my wife's muff, spurting his thick white gravy deep inside her. *"Fuck...DAMMIT!!!"*

"Quiet!" I press a finger over my lips as I whisper loudly. Their bodies writhe around on top of the desk as they finish in each other's arms. Todd eventually pulls out of Sophie and a stream of white semen slowly makes its way out of her and onto my desk.

"Damn, that was good." Todd stands back and looks down at his wilting pecker. "I have never been with a woman like you."

My wife stands up and puts on her skirt. Only now do I realize that she was not wearing underwear when she came into my office earlier. "Yeah, thanks." Sophis puts on her bra and blouse quietly as she looks away from us.

"Was it really okay?" Todd asks her.

"Yeah, it was great. Really." My wife barely looks at him as she finishes getting dressed. She then walks calmly to my office door and leaves without saying another word.

"Um, what?" Todd looks over at me.

"I don't know what's going on." My cock is still hard and the front of my pants are wet with pre-come. Though I did not get off with my wife, I still feel as if I need a cigarette and a small glass of scotch.

"I didn't make her mad, did I?"

"No, I don't think so," I tell him. "Go ahead and get dressed before someone comes in here, Todd." He does as I ask and once done he has a seat in front of me. A small glob of his DNA still rests on my desktop between us. "Sorry about that," he says while reaching for a Kleenex.

"It's fine," I tell him. "I have sanitizing wipes in the cabinet." As I study his face, I ask, "Was she everything that you thought she would be?"

He chuckles. "And then some, man. Damn, your wife can make up her mind quickly, huh?"

"Yes she can," I reply. "Though, I think she probably had already decided that she was going to have sex with you before she got here."

"I got that feeling too," he replies. "Fuck, man. You are one lucky asshole, Ollie. She's a fiery kitten."

"Thanks." I laugh a little as I think about the next story I will write and upload to the forums. Now that the admin has decided to leave up my stories, I guess I will play along.

"I've got a thing, so..." Todd gets up and wipes the dollop of his white sauce from my desk. After tossing the used Kleenex into my trash can, he walks to the office door and leaves. It takes only a moment of thought before I turn to my computer and pull up the forums where I have posted the stories about my wife's alter-ego, Sophia.

"This is going to be hot," I say to myself as I begin typing. Maybe I should be worried that the IT department will pick up on what I am doing, especially since this particular website is supposed to be blocked by the server in the building. Todd has promised me that there is a guy on the inside who will shield me from any problems. I have no clue who that is, but I am putting my career in his hands as I write the next story about my wife getting fucked on my desk.

Chapter Ten: Worth It

"You confused us a little when you left so suddenly," I tell Sophie as I walk into our house. She is sitting on the sofa with a cup of hot tea in her hands.

"I went ahead and took the whole day off," she says while avoiding answering my comment. "It's been nice to take some time to myself."

"Yeah, I'll bet," I chuckle. "Honestly, though, what do you think about what happened? Was it okay or are you sorry that it happened?"

My wife turns to look at me with her bright blue eyes. "Why would I be sorry for that? I started it, didn't I?" She smugly smiles at me before turning her attention back to her cup of tea and taking a drink. I get the distinct feeling that Sophie is proud of the way she handled herself with Todd in my office today.

"You look pretty confident about the whole thing, I have to admit, honey. I just want to be certain that you and I are just fine after you did that with him. Did you like it?"

Sophie nods her head and smiles. "I really did. Ollie, I didn't think that I could do that, even after coming to your office this morning, but then something inside me said to just go with it." Her face turns a little red as she admits, "I liked that you were there watching me. It helped me to get off."

"I'm not sure you would have had any trouble getting off with Todd this morning, even if I hadn't been there," I laugh. "The two of you together were pretty electric."

"He's got a wild way about him."

"Yes he does," I answer with a smile. "The guy is really good with women."

"Then why doesn't he have a wife?" she asks. "You would think that a guy who could pay that kind of attention to a woman would have found someone by now."

I shrug my shoulders. "I think that's why he hasn't found someone. To Todd, it's all about sex. There's no love there from him for the woman he is with. Just hard, sweaty sex." My cock gets a little hard again as I think of Sophie with my friend earlier in the day. It was a sight to behold as I watched the two of them together.

"You want more, don't you?" she asks.

Nodding my head, I ask, "Would you want to have sex with Todd again? Not tonight, but you know, sometime in the future?" We both laugh a little as her blue eyes look away from me for a moment.

"Maybe."

"That's your favorite word, isn't it?" I ask my wife.

"Which one? Maybe?"

"Yeah, that one. I think you've used it with me in regards to all this maybe a dozen or so times. *Maybe.*" We both laugh again. There is a nervousness between me and my wife of almost ten years. We know each other so well, but then again there is still so much more to learn about ourselves.

"It's hard for me to be absolute sometimes," Sophie explains. "I get nervous when something has to do with sex. You know that. The fact that Todd and I got together today is a huge deal for me. Ollie, you have no idea how hard that was for me. I almost didn't do it. I almost told you to keep that guy away from me from now on."

"Oh? So, that's a *no* on seeing him again?"

"I'm not saying that," she replies. "I just want you to know that everything has to be on my terms if this is going to happen again."

"I see. So, you see yourself doing this again?" I am pressing her, but I feel that I have to if I am going to get a straight answer from my wife.

Sophie smiles. "Probably with Todd again and then maybe we can talk about what happens after him."

Goosebumps rise along my arms and neck. "Do you mean to say that you want to have sex with other men as well?

She shrugs her shoulders. "Isn't that what you ultimately want out of all this? To see me have sex with more than one guy over a period of time? You have written about it, after all."

"Well, sure," I admit. "Isn't that what any red-blooded male wants to see?" We laugh together for a moment as I reach over and touch my wife's knee. "I just want you to be alright with it all, honey. Don't let me push you too far. You know as well as I that if you feel trapped you tend to get a little mean."

"Yeah, don't push me," she replies. "Just let things happen naturally. Like I said, I want control over when and how things happen. Since it's my body, that's fair, right?"

"It's fair," I agree.

"Then, maybe Saturday evening would be a good time to have Todd over. I feel like that would be a good time for me to have a little more fun with him."

"Tomorrow night? Really?" She nods her head and I feel my cock stiffen. "He'll be really happy to hear that, Sophie."

"Good. Let him know, but tell him that it will be at my pace. I don't want him trying to seduce me or anything like that. Oh, and get some good wine."

I raise an eyebrow. "Good *wine?* Are you telling me that you want alcohol Saturday night while he is here?"

"Sure. Get some good stuff. Maybe some port."

"Um, alright." I smile nervously as I think about what will happen with alcohol freely flowing in our house on Saturday night with Todd here.

"I'm going to go take a quick shower. I still have some of your friend left on me." Sophie points toward her crotch and I feel my shaft stiffen yet again. She appears to notice, but says nothing as she gets up and walks back to the bedroom with her cup of hot tea.

Pulling out my cell phone, I quickly message my friend. "Todd, boy are you going to be a happy guy."

A moment later, he texts back. "In what way?"

"Saturday night. Let's say sevenish. Sophie wants you over at our house, alright?"

"Seriously? Tomorrow night?"

"Yep." I send a devilish emoji as I stand to my feet. I am so fucking excited that I need to walk back and forth in the living room to work off some of the extra energy that I am finding myself with.

"Damn, man. I'll be there. Are we having Chinese again?"

"Wine," I reply. "Port wine. I'm going to get a couple of bottles. It's Sophie's idea."

"Damn." I get the sense that Todd is smiling widely right now. After all, this is far more than he had probably expected.

"Tell him to bring a suitcase," I hear Sophie call out from the bedroom. Apparently she figures that I am texting with him even though she has not come out here to see me doing it. "He's staying the night."

"Fuck," I say to myself before I relay the message. "Pack a bag, Todd," I tell him in a text message. "Sophie wants you to stay all night. Just remember that it's her show, though. She has the say when and how things happen."

I hear back almost instantly. "Tell her that I will do whatever I have to do to enjoy her again, Ollie. Anything. Anything at all." He sends a list of emojis that appear to be a united effort to show me just how happy my friend is at this time.

"I thought you would like that. Just get here showered and shaved and ready. I'm not sure what will happen." I send my last message to him and put my phone away. I cannot believe all that has happened over the last couple of weeks. For a while I was posting my fantasy stories on a website that would become the center of a contentious marital crisis for me and my wife. Now Sophie and I are in agreement to bring other men into the relationship occasionally so that I can enjoy seeing her with them. Though she might make this out to be a favor to me, my wife has also intimated that she liked fucking Todd. Therefore, I have to think that she will enjoy tomorrow night as well. I am not sure where we will find the other men she has spoken of, but Sophie might already have an idea as to who that should be. All I ask is that I am a part of it when she decides that she is ready for the next one. I will be there and ready to watch.

THE END

Don't miss out!

Visit the website below and you can sign up to receive emails whenever Karly Violet publishes a new book. There's no charge and no obligation.

https://books2read.com/r/B-A-GIXE-FZHMB

BOOKS 2 READ

Connecting independent readers to independent writers.

Did you love *Hotwife Fantasy Comes True - A Steamy Romance Hot Wife Novel*? Then you should read *Hotwife Affair In Lockdown - A Hotwife Multiple Partner Wife Watching Romance Novel*[1] by Karly Violet!

[2]

Beautiful Wife Finds A Way To Comfort Her Loneliness During The Pandemic While Her Husband Is Stranded Overseas

The early stages of the pandemic **separated many married couples.**

And this was no different for Leyland and his wife Karie.

The successful husband was travelling on business from the States to London.

But as he neared the end of his trip and the pandemic was gripping the world, non-essential flights were grounded and Leyland found himself stranded thousands of miles away from his beautiful wife.

---

1. https://books2read.com/u/3JRB6A

2. https://books2read.com/u/3JRB6A

The uncertainty of when Leyland would return back home didn't concern him, he knew their marriage would strengthen further.

Karie believed this too...........**until she started to get lonely.**

And the longer Leyland was away, the more the **stunning housewife yearned for intimacy.**

So much so that neighbours started to notice as men started to visit Karie almost daily.

Can a lonely housewife's cheating ways ever be forgiven?

This 20,000 word scorching hot novel features a lonely wife exploring way to comfort her loneliness whilst her husband is stranded overseas in the midst of the pandemic!

Read more at https://www.patreon.com/karlyviolet.

About the Author

Sign up to my mailing list to receive the two free epilogues for 'A Hotwife Adventure' and 'Hotwife Training' and to stay up to date on all of my latest releases! http://eepurl.com/c3ICWf Sign up to my Patreon account and receive exclusive Hotwife stories every month and sexy scenes every week! https://www.patreon.com/karlyviolet

Read more at https://www.patreon.com/karlyviolet.

About the Publisher